KT-557-126

Fife
COUNCIL
Fife Council Education Department
King's Road Primary School
King's Crescent, Rosyth KY11 2RS

The Seal Hunter

Other brilliant stories to collect:

Aesop's Fables
Malorie Blackman

Hansel and Gretel
Henrietta Branford

The Goose Girl
Gillian Cross

The Snow Queen
Berlie Doherty

The Twelve Dancing Princesses
Anne Fine

Grey Wolf, Prince Jack and the Firebird
Alan Garner

The Three Heads in the Well
Susan Gates

The Six Swan Brothers
Adèle Geras

Cockadoodle-doo, Mr Sultana!
Michael Morpurgo

Mossycoat
Philip Pullman

Rapunzel
Jacqueline Wilson

Rumpelstiltskin
Kit Wright

The Seal Hunter

Retold by
Tony Mitton

Illustrated by
Nick Maland

SCHOLASTIC
Home of the Story

Scholastic Children's Books,
Commonwealth House, 1–19 New Oxford Street,
London WC1A 1NU, UK
a division of Scholastic Ltd
London ~ New York ~ Toronto ~ Sydney ~ Auckland
Mexico City ~ New Delhi ~ Hong Kong

First published by Scholastic Ltd, 1998

ISBN 0 590 54390 3

Printed by Cox and Wyman Ltd, Reading, Berks.

4 6 8 10 9 7 5

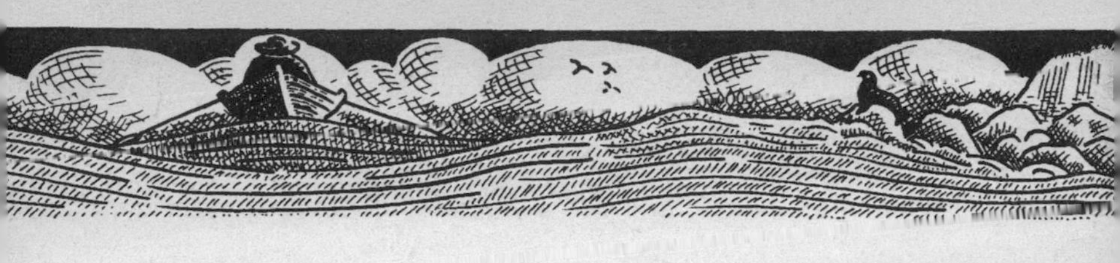

For David Fickling,
gratefully
T.M.

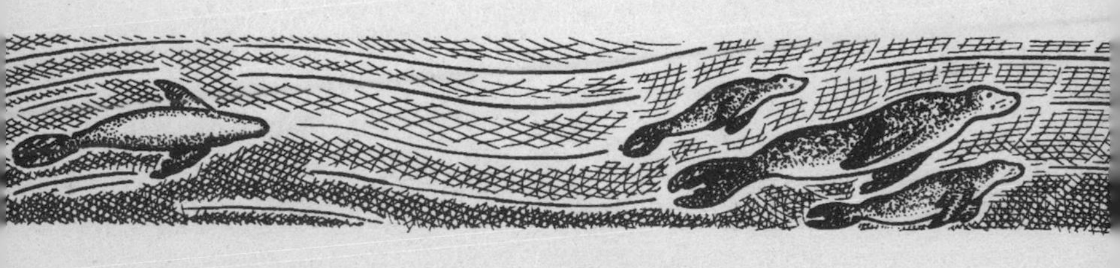

Here is a story handed down
from many a year ago.
The tale's been told by many a tongue
but I shall tell it so.

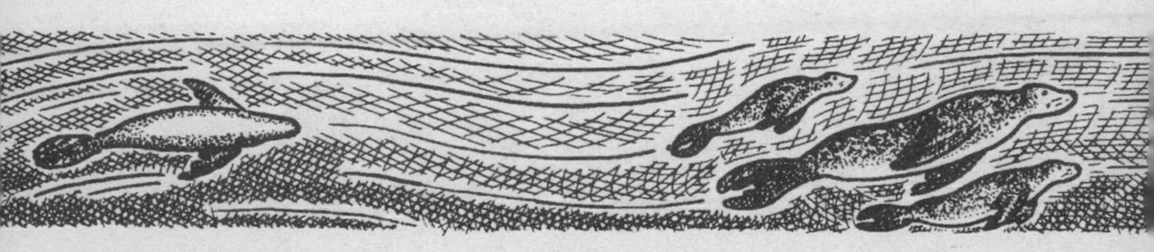

Duncan MacKinnon was a fisherman.
He sold his catch for a fee.
He lived in a lonely stone-built croft
by the side of the ragged sea.

And when he could, he would hunt
the seals
and strip them of their hides.
He would keep and cure each
precious pelt
but throw each corpse to the tides.

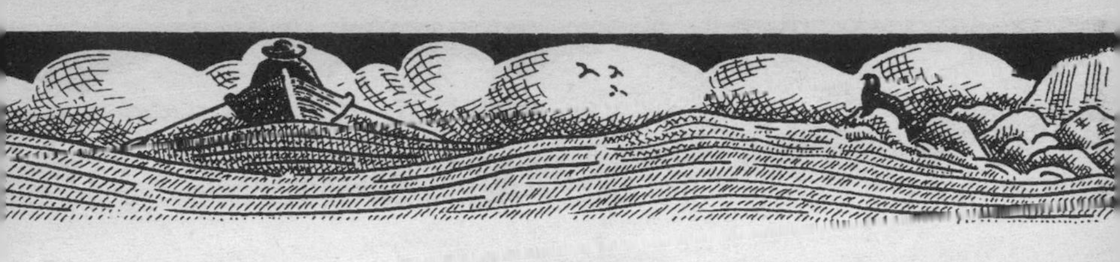

Now in those days the pelts were
prized
and folk would pay full well
for a sealskin cap, or a bag, or boots,
or clothes, as I've heard tell.

And the local folk came knocking
at the sealskin seller's door,
so in time he left his floats and nets
and hunted seals the more.

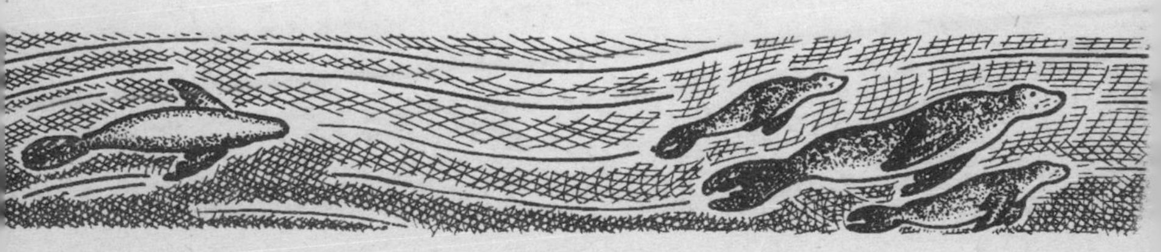

Duncan MacKinnon rowed the tides.
At his belt he wore a knife.
And with the aid of its deadly blade
he would take each sad seal's life.

The hunter soon grew stout and rich
with the sale of the skins he caught.
He lived his life by the skill of his
knife,
but gave the seals small thought.

It was on a day, in a sunlit bay,
when the whole sea seemed to smile,
he sighted a huge and handsome seal
stretched out on a rocky isle.

When he saw the size of the great,
grey seal
he crooned, "With a skin like that
you could trim and shape a costly
cape
or many a shoe and hat."

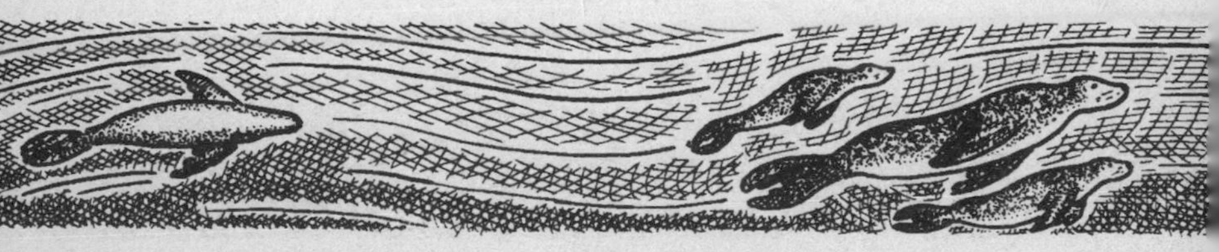

So he moored his boat but a short
    way off
and he crept up, yard by yard.
Then, almost there, he leaped
    through the air
and he drove his knife in hard.

But the great, grey seal was a fighter,
and he writhed from the hunter's
    grip.
With the knife in his side he dived for
    the tide
and he gave his man the slip.

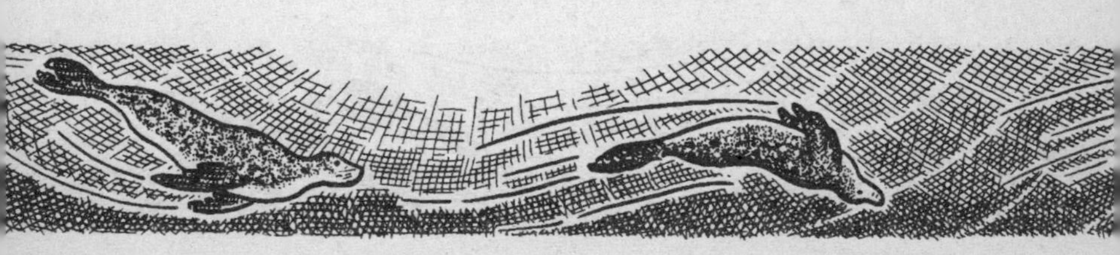

MacKinnon shrugged and returned to his boat
to row to his own home shore.
"The seals in the sea swim wide and free,"
he mused. "There are plenty more."

Duncan MacKinnon, oh, Duncan
MacKinnon,
now take great heed, beware.
The fill of a purse can be a curse
for living things to bear.

The clink of a coin and its comfort
may keep you warm and dry.
But what of the shame that sticks to your
name
at each sad creature's cry?

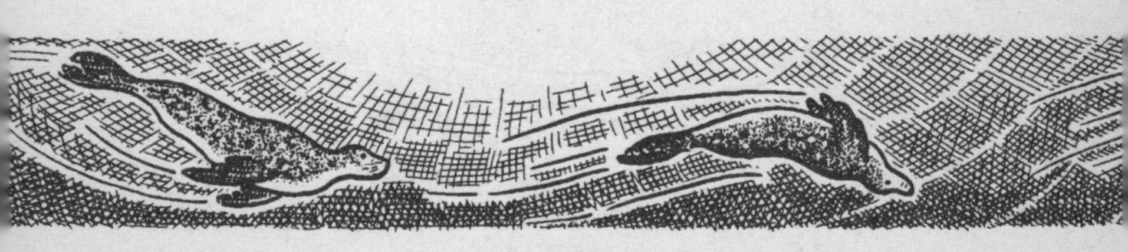

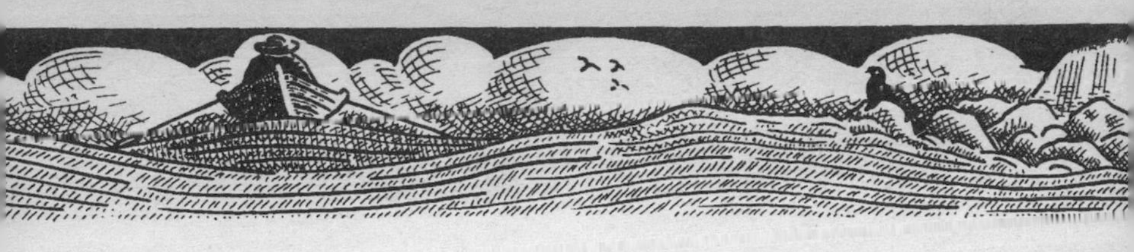

What is the worth of a wealth that's
ripped
from the world by a ruthless knife?
What of the guilt on which it's built
as you strip each struggling life?

Duncan MacKinnon, when you were a
boy,
did you never sit down on the beach
to learn from the pound of the stern
sea-sound
the lessons that it might teach?

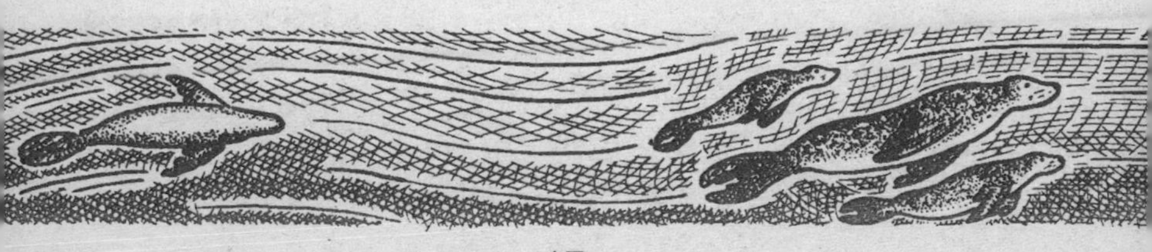

Faithless fisherman, when you were young,
did nobody think to tell
that there's more in the sea than a hunter's
fee,
there's life in the great grey swell?

Did nobody show you, upon the shore,
when you were both young and small,
that the rolling sea, so fair and free,
is the Ancient Mother of All?

Sad seal hunter, learn in time,
as you stack your brimming store,
when simple need grows into greed
there'll be darkness at your door.

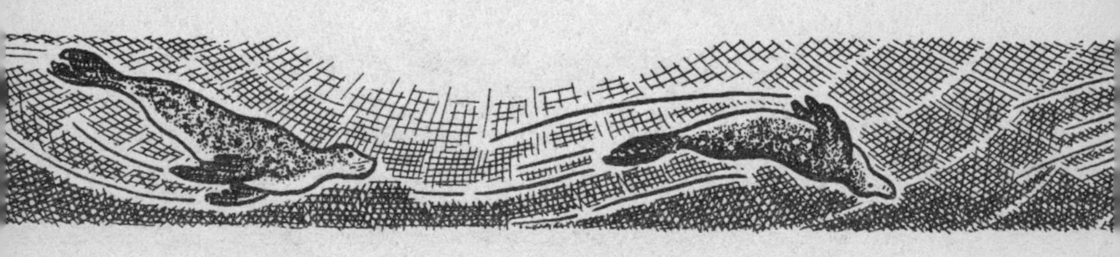

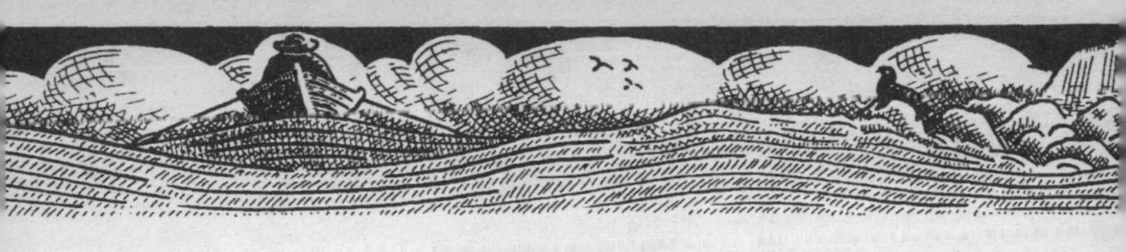

Late that night, as he sat by the light
of his guttering oil-lamp flame,
there came a knock at his low croft
door
and a voice called out his name.

In a place so lone, at an hour so late,
who could this caller be?
The curious hunter loosed the door
and peered out cautiously.

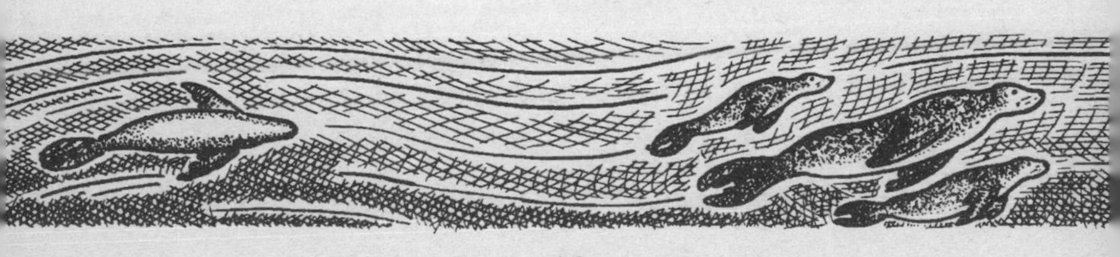

There on the threshold stood a man
in a cape both dark and long.
He spoke to the wary hunter
in a deep voice, soft yet strong.

"Duncan MacKinnon, say, is it so,
you have seal skins here to sell?
Are you that famous hunter
of whom the folk all tell?"

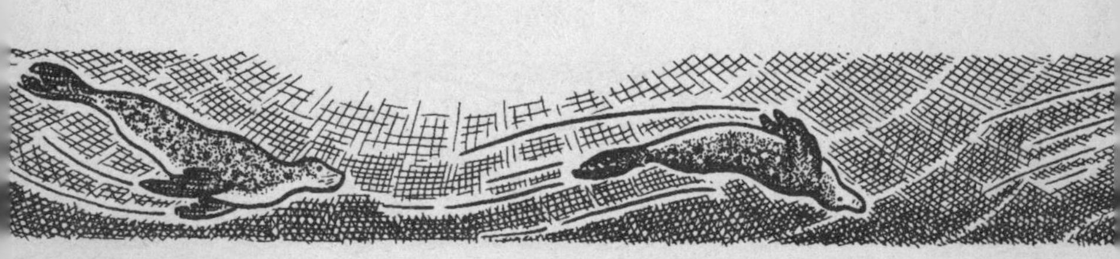

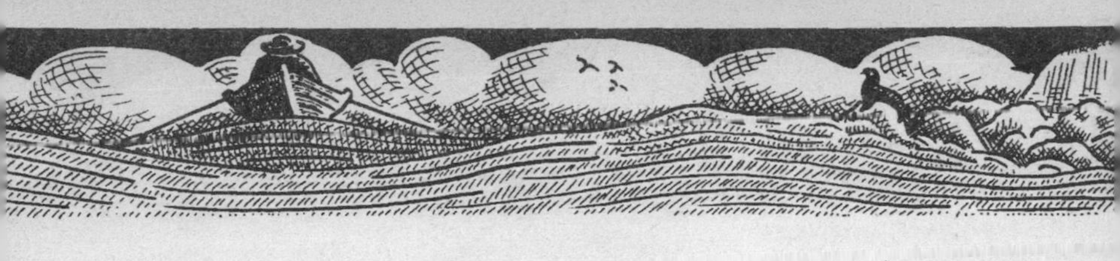

Duncan MacKinnon nodded.
"Of skins I have full store.
I'll sell you all the skins you need.
The sea holds plenty more."

The dark-caped stranger listened
to the words the hunter told.
"My master waits nearby," he said,
"if you wish your skins all sold."

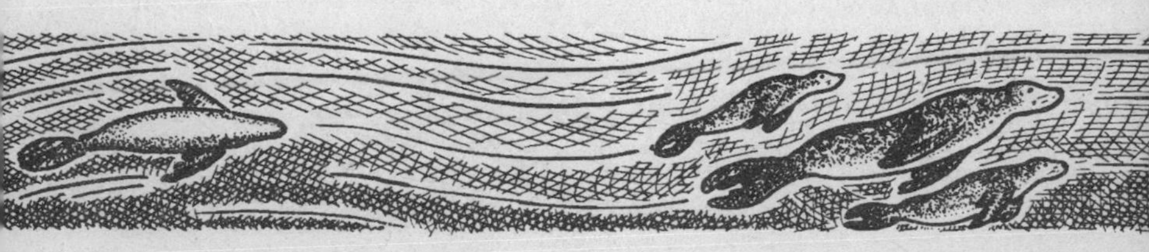

Duncan MacKinnon and the stranger
walked out to the edge of the land.
"Now where," said the man, "is my
master?
He was here just now, at hand..."

They peered at the edge of the
clifftop
where the brink might break and slip.
It was then that the hunter felt his
arms
held tight in a vice-like grip.

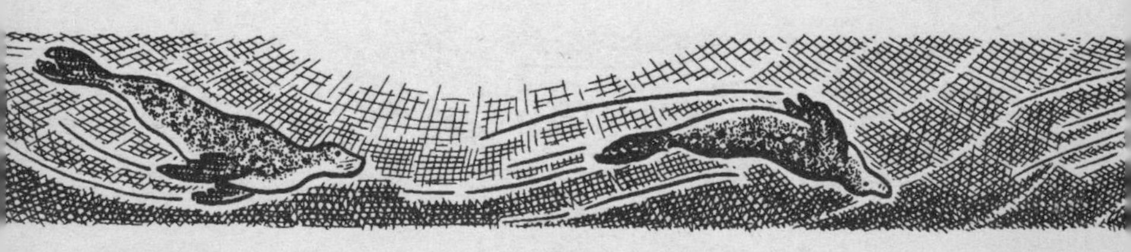

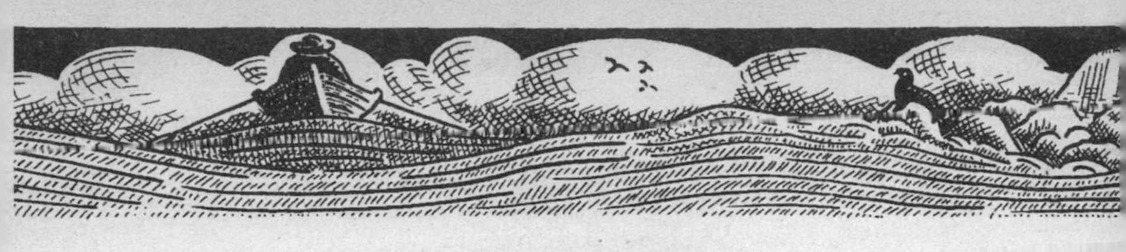

And before he could make a murmur
or shake his pinned arms free,
the stranger leaped from the clifftop
and they plummeted down to the sea.

As they hit the cold and dark of the
waves
the stranger pulled him down.
The hunter felt his life was done,
for now he must surely drown.

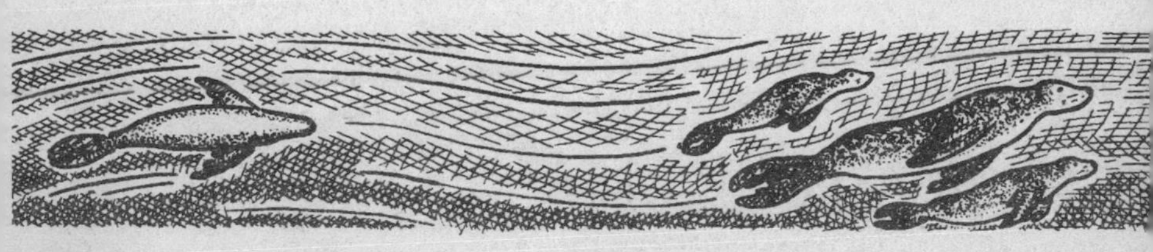

Down they went, far deep beneath
the foam and the rolling waves,
till they came to an underwater
world
where the rocks were pierced with
caves.

Still he felt the stranger's hands
where they gripped his arms so tight,
as together they swam through the
mouth of a cave
and into a greeny light.

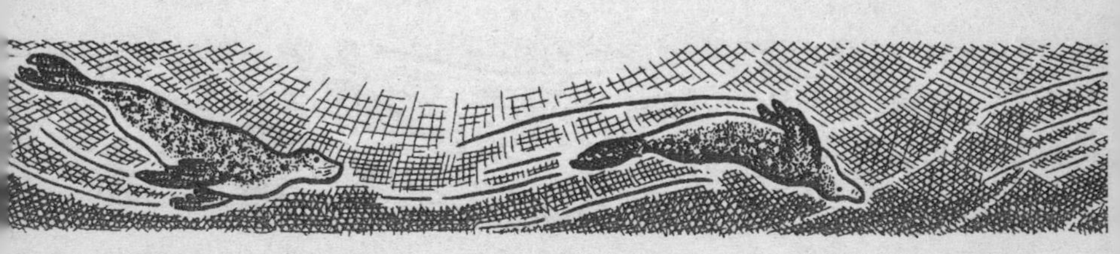

And down in that weird and greeny
light
where he thought to meet his death,
when his will gave way and he drank
the brine
he found he could draw his breath.

Now as he drank that liquid brine
he felt both light and free.
And the eerie glide of his sinister ride
seemed neither of land nor sea.

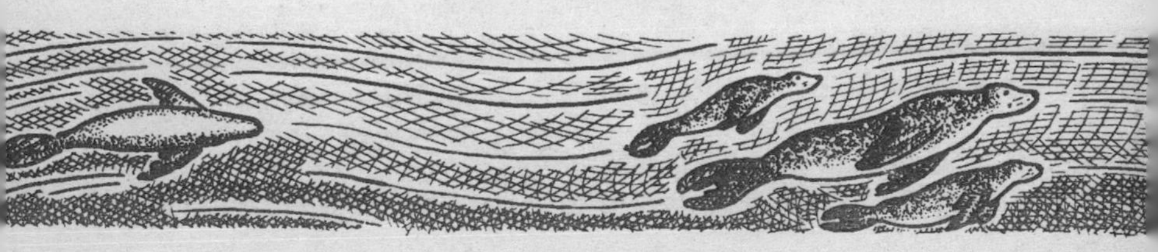

It was then that he noticed the skin
of his guide
had a silky, a slippery feel.
In the watery light he saw to his
fright
that the man had become a seal.

Gone were the hands and gone were
the feet,
and gone was the long, black cape.
For now the dark guide that he
floated beside
was wholly a seal in shape.

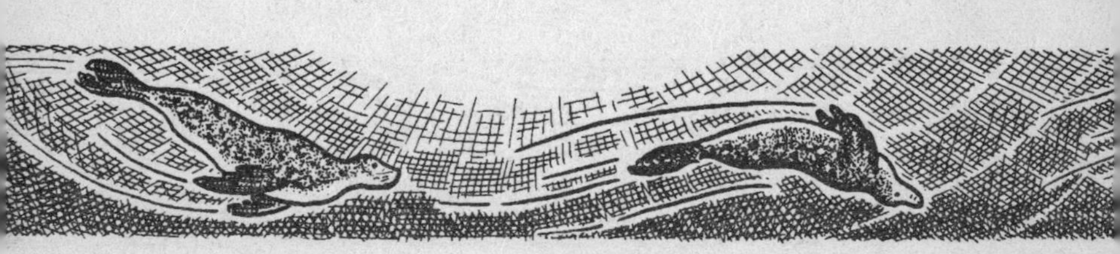

His silent seal-guide drew him on
to an underwater town
where the walls shone white with a
    pearly light
and the seals swam up and down.

They swam till they came to a palace
and they passed on through its door.
And once inside his eyes went wide
at the sight the hunter saw.

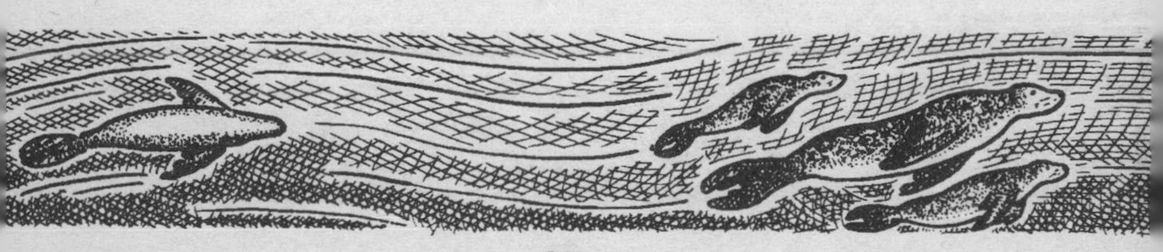

There were white rock seats in a circle
where many a seal sat round.
But in that solemn circus
there came not ever a sound.

For there in the circle's centre,
set out on a white rock bed,
lay a seal so still and silent
it seemed that seal lay dead.

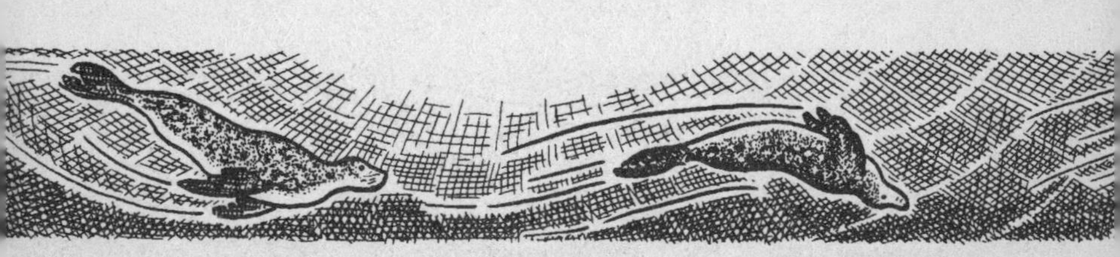

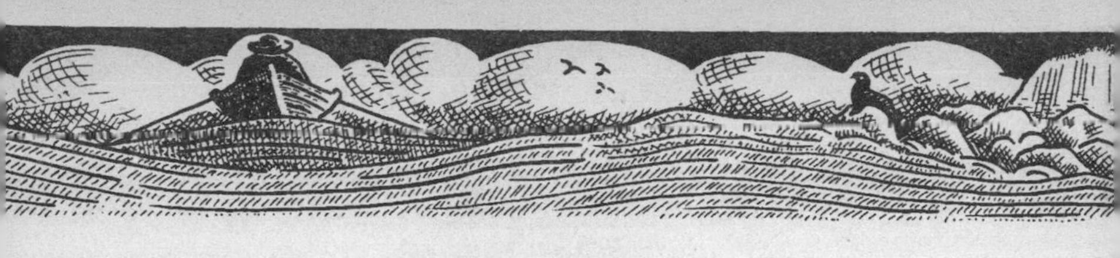

Then the hunter saw the knife in its
side
and he opened his mouth to moan.
There on its hilt was the ring of gilt
that marked it as his own.

He fell to his knees on the chamber
floor
and wrung his hands in fear.
Alone, deep down in the selkie town
he sensed his end was near.

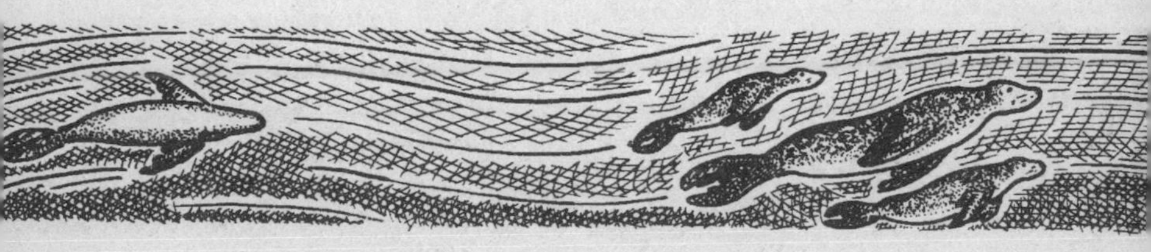

But the seal-guide's voice spoke up to
him
and seemed to fill his head.
"Remove the knife and smoothe the
wound,"
that strange voice softly said.

The hunter pulled his cruel knife out
and wiped its blade of steel.
When, with his hand, he smoothed
the wound,
he saw it swiftly heal.

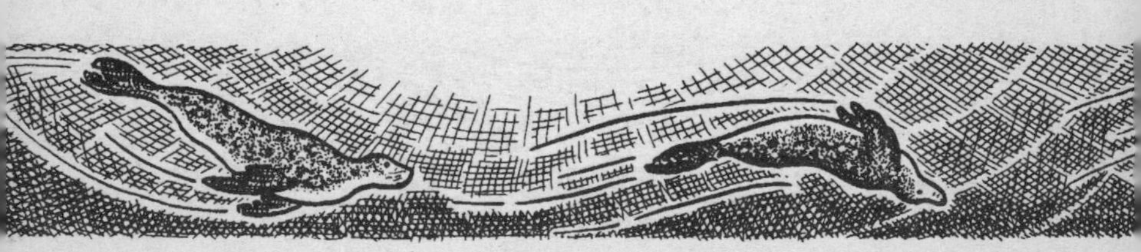

The great seal stirred and seemed to
stretch,
then reared up proud and high.
He turned toward the hunter
and fixed him with his eye.

"I am the King of the Seals," he said.
"Your seal-guide is my son.
The time has come to settle up
the deeds that you have done.

"Tonight my son has brought you here
to gather back your knife.
And if you now repent your deeds
I'll grant you back your life.

"If you will fish the seas again
and do the seals no ill,
we seals will always be your friends
and help your nets to fill.

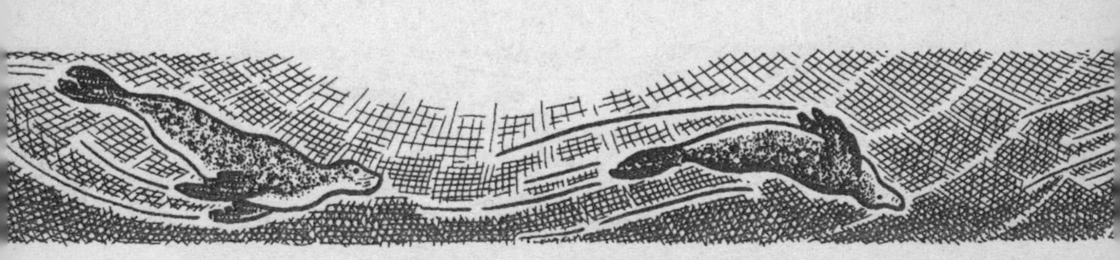

"But if you slay a seal once more
and take it for its skin,
the Selkie Folk will seek you out
and slay you for your sin.

"Now stand again, and sheathe your
knife
and say before us now,
will you give up the hunter's life
and take the Selkie Vow?"

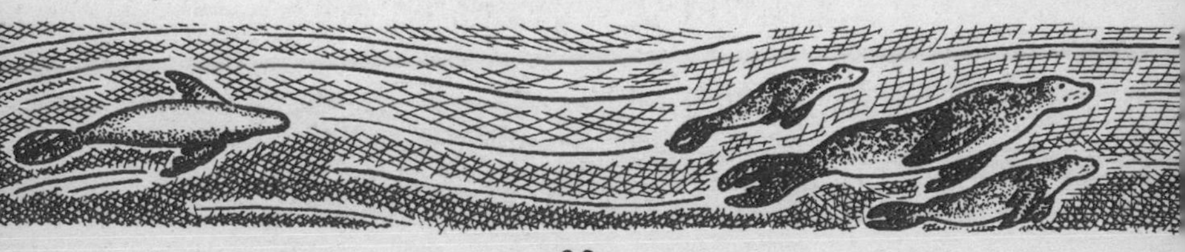

The hunter rose and sheathed his
knife,
then, there upon the sand,
he saw appear these words so clear,
as if by secret hand:

I, who live by swell of sea,
will learn to use it modestly,
to fish it but for honest need,
and not to grasp with rising greed.

I, who ride on wealth of wave,
will vow to cherish, succour, save,
never to pluck or cruelly plunder
what goes over, on or under.

I, who tell the turning tide,
will make the sea my place, my pride,
and guard all things that go within,
whether of scale or shell or skin.

I, who live beside the shore,
will know content, not ask for more.
I am for her, and she for me.
The Selkie Vow respects The Sea.

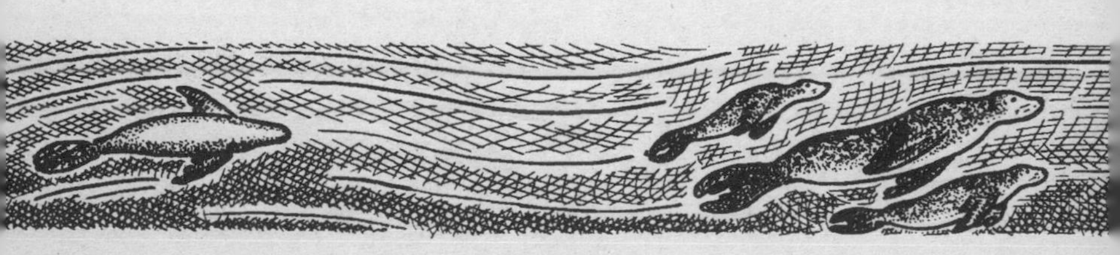

The hunter stood and took the Vow
and at each word he spoke
the darkness seemed to gather round
and wrap him like a cloak.

He fell into a deep sea swoon
where waters rolled him round.
And when he woke it seemed to him
he lay on solid ground.

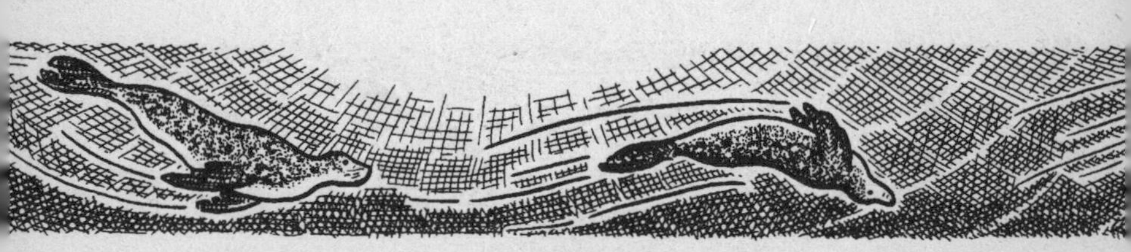

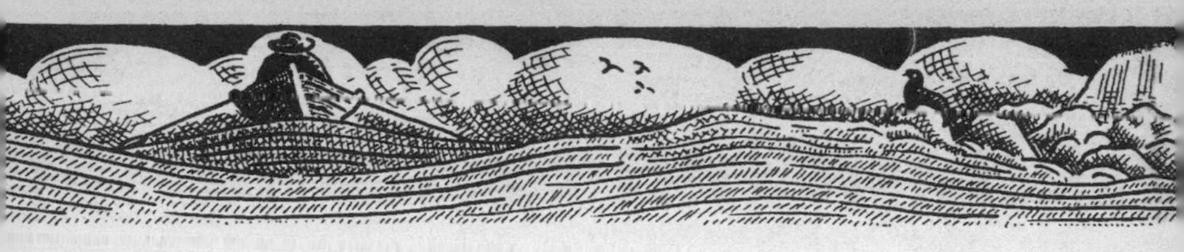

He raised his head and looked about.
The moon shone sweet and soft.
Above him on the cliff he saw
his stony fisher-croft.

He climbed the path and found his
door,
then stumbled to his bed.
And all that night the strange events
went reeling through his head.

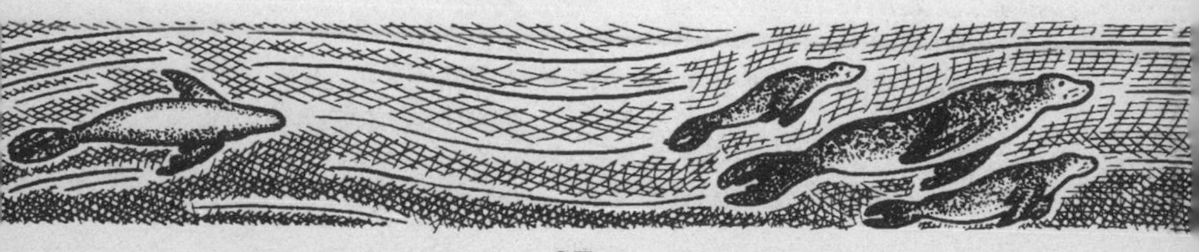

But when the light of early dawn
came trickling through his pane
he rose to fetch his fishing nets
and cast them once again.

And, from that time, if traders,
skin dealers, came to call,
he'd show them where his dagger
hung,
sheathed safely on the wall.

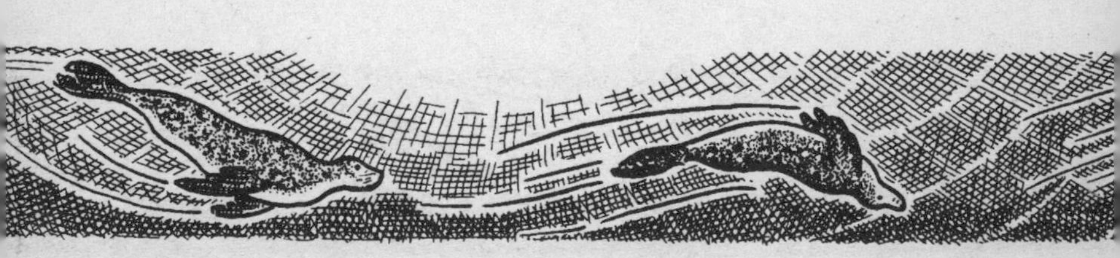

He'd sit them at his table
and tell his story through,
of how he met the Selkie Folk,
and the king he nearly slew.

And how once more he fished the sea
and looked to it for life,
but never more would harm a seal
with net or club or knife.

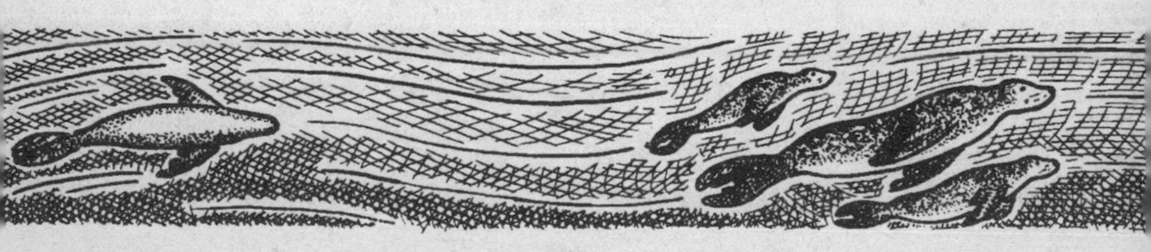

And how, whenever he rode the waves,
in swollen tides or calm,
his nets were never empty
and he never came to harm.

My story's done and over,
my tale is at an end,
of how a cruel hunter
became the selkies' friend.

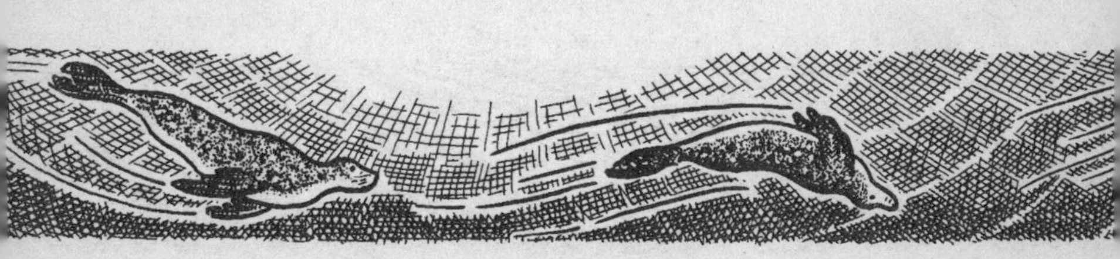

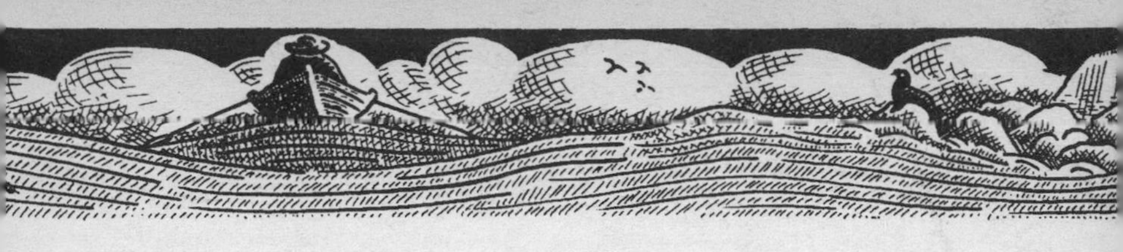

It is a story handed down
from many a year ago.
The tale's been told by many a tongue,
but I have told it so.

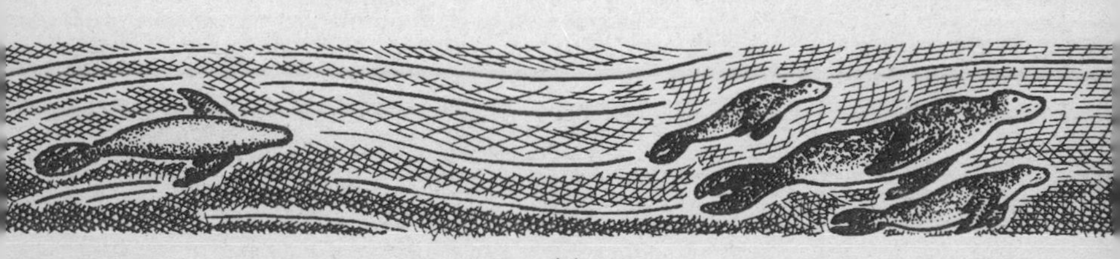

Other stories to collect:

Aesop's Fables

Malorie Blackman

Illustrated by Patrice Aggs

Once upon a time there was a man named Aesop who told stories full of wisdom...

Hansel and Gretel

Henrietta Branford

Illustrated by Lesley Harker

Once upon a time there were a brother and sister who were left alone in the forest...

The Snow Queen

Berlie Doherty

Illustrated by Siân Bailey

Once upon a time there was a little boy whose heart was turned to ice...

The Twelve Dancing Princesses

Anne Fine

Illustrated by Debi Gliori

Once upon a time there were twelve princesses, and no one knew why their shoes were full of holes...

Grey Wolf, Prince Jack and the Firebird

Alan Garner

Illustrated by James Mayhew

Once upon a time there was a prince who set out to seek the mysterious firebird...

Mossycoat

Philip Pullman

Illustrated by Peter Bailey

Once upon a time there was a beautiful girl whose mother made her a magical, mossy coat...

The Six Swan Brothers

Adèle Geras

Illustrated by Ian Beck

Once upon a time there was a brave princess who saw her six brothers turned into swans...

The Three Heads in the Well

Susan Gates

Illustrated by Sue Heap

Once upon a time there were two stepsisters – one good, one bad – who both went out to seek their fortunes...

Cockadoodle-doo, Mr Sultana!

Michael Morpurgo

Illustrated by Michael Foreman

Once upon a time there was a rich and greedy sultan who met a clever little cockerel...

Rapunzel

Jacqueline Wilson

Illustrated by Nick Sharratt

Once upon a time there was a baby who was stolen by a witch...

Rumpelstiltskin

Kit Wright

Illustrated by Ted Dewan

Once upon a time there was a beautiful girl who would die if she couldn't spin straw into gold...

The Goose Girl

Gillian Cross

Illustrated by Jason Cockcroft

Once upon a time there was a princess who lost everything she had ever owned...